Peas and Potatoes, 1, 2, 3

Written by Michael K. Smith
Illustrated by Benrei Huang

STECK-VAUGHN
C O M P A N Y

A Division of Harcourt Brace & Company

The hungry mole eats one cabbage.

2

The hungry mole eats two onions.

The hungry mole eats three potatoes.

4

The hungry mole eats four pea pods.

The hungry mole eats five beans.

The hungry mole eats six carrots.

The full mole takes a long nap!